WELCOME TO
PASSPORT TO READING
A beginning reader's ticket to a brand-new world!

Every book in this program is designed to build read-along and read-alone skills, level by level, through engaging and enriching stories. As the reader turns each page, he or she will become more confident with new vocabulary, sight words, and comprehension.

These PASSPORT TO READING levels will help you choose the perfect book for every reader.

READING TOGETHER
Read short words in simple sentence structures together to begin a reader's journey.

READING OUT LOUD
Encourage developing readers to sound out words in more complex stories with simple vocabulary.

READING INDEPENDENTLY
Newly independent readers gain confidence reading more complex sentences with higher word counts.

READY TO READ MORE
Readers prepare for chapter books with fewer illustrations and longer paragraphs.

This book features sight words from the educator-supported Dolch Sight Words List. This encourages the reader to recognize commonly used vocabulary words, increasing reading speed and fluency.

For more information, please visit www.passporttoreadingbooks.com.

Enjoy the journey!

Little, Brown and Company

Hachette Book Group
237 Park Avenue, New York, NY 10017
Visit our website at www.lb-kids.com

Little, Brown and Company is a division of Hachette Book Group, Inc.
The Little, Brown name and logo are trademarks of Hachette Book Group, Inc.

The publisher is not responsible for websites (or their content)
that are not owned by the publisher.

First Edition: April 2013

ISBN 978-0-316-18315-4

Library of Congress Control Number: 2012942751

Book design by Maria Mercado

10 9 8 7 6 5 4 3 2 1

CW

Printed in the United States of America

Passport to Reading titles are leveled by independent reviewers applying the standards developed by Irene Fountas and Gay Su Pinnell in *Matching Books to Readers: Using Leveled Books in Guided Reading*, Heinemann, 1999.

THE MUPPETS

Fozzie's Funny Business

by Martha T. Ottersley

illustrated by James Silvani

LITTLE, BROWN AND COMPANY
New York   Boston

Hi, Muppet fans!

Can you find these things in this book?

BANANA PEEL

TISSUE

DRUMS

Every day at the Muppet Theater,
the Muppets get lots of mail.
Most of it is from fans all over the world.
All the Muppets love getting letters.

Some envelopes just have bills
that need to be paid.
No one loves getting bills.

A lot of the fan mail is for Animal.

The fan letters say things such as,

"Animal is so funny!"

and "Animal makes us laugh!"

Fozzie Bear reads some of the letters
before Animal eats them.
The letters give Fozzie an idea.
"Everyone thinks Animal is funny," says Fozzie.
"If I put him in my comedy act,
then maybe everyone will think I am funnier!"

Fozzie decides to give his idea a try.
He asks Animal to practice with him
while the other Muppets watch.
"After I tell a joke about snow,"
says Fozzie, "you sprinkle snow on me."
"Snow! Snow!" Animal shouts.

"Where does a snowman go to dance?" asks Fozzie.

"A snow*ball*, get it?

Wocka! Wocka!"

Animal dumps a pail of snow on Fozzie!

The other Muppets laugh out loud.

Fozzie dusts the snow off and tries again.

"Now I am going to tell a banana joke,"
Fozzie tells Animal.

"Just peel this banana and then throw the peel."

"Throw peel! Throw peel!" shouts Animal.

"Why did the banana go to the doctor?" asks Fozzie.

"Because he was not *peeling* well—ha ha!"

Before Fozzie even finishes laughing,

Animal throws the banana peel.

It lands right in front of the bear.
Fozzie slips on it and slides across the floor,
crashing into the costume closet. WHAM!
Everyone laughs again.

This is not going the way Fozzie expected,

but he will not give up.

He hands Animal a dozen eggs.

"When I say 'now,' you slowly toss me an egg.

Got it?"

"Egg toss! Egg toss!" shouts Animal.

"Why should you never tell jokes to eggs?"
asks Fozzie.

"Now, Animal!" he whispers.

Animal throws one egg to Fozzie.

Then another, and another, and another!

Fozzie cannot catch them.

Soon he is covered in broken eggs.

"Because they might *crack up*,"
says an egg-soaked Fozzie.

Everyone laughs again.

Fozzie cleans himself up.

"Maybe using props is not your thing,"
Fozzie says to Animal.

"Let us try something else.

How about a knock-knock joke?

When I say 'Knock, knock,'

you say 'Who is there?'

Are you ready?"

"Ready!" says Animal.

"Knock, knock," says Fozzie.

Animal is supposed to say "Who is there?"

But instead, he runs to the door and answers it.

It is Scooter, with more fan mail for Animal!

"Knock, knock," Fozzie begins.

"Who there?" Animal asks.

"Watch!" Fozzie says.

"Watch who!?"

Animal sneezes.

It is a real sneeze!

And a big one!

It sends Fozzie sailing across the room

and right into the wig closet!

Everyone roars with laughter.

"This act is not going to work," says Fozzie.
"Animal just will not do these jokes
the way I want him to."
"If you want your act to sing,
you let Animal do his thing,"
says Floyd Pepper.

"Excuse me, Floyd,
but what does that mean?" asks Fozzie.
"It means, do not be bummed,
just let him hit his drums!" says Floyd.
"If you say so," says Fozzie.

It is almost time for the show to start.

"Get ready, everyone," Kermit says.

Fozzie feels a little nervous

as Scooter puts Animal's drums on the stage.

What will Animal do this time?

The show must go on!
The curtain opens,
and Fozzie starts his first joke.

"What do tiny elves make sandwiches with?"
Fozzie asks the audience.

"*Short*bread! Wocka! Wocka!"

Animal plays the drums. BA-DUM CRASH!

The audience starts to giggle.

Fozzie realizes that hearing the drums
lets the audience know it is time to laugh!
"How can you tell the ocean is friendly?"
Fozzie asks with a big smile.
"Because it *waves*!"

Animal bangs his drums again.
BA-DUM CRASH!
The audience laughs out loud!

"What did planet Mars say to planet Saturn?"
Fozzie asks.

"'How about giving me a *ring* sometime?'
Wocka! Wocka!"

Animal plays. BA-DUM CRASH!

The audience laughs again, even harder.

"Animal," Fozzie whispers,
"this is the best show ever,
thanks to you and your drumming!
Will you always play drums with me
when I do my act?"
"Play drums!" yells Animal.

After the performance,
Scooter finds Fozzie backstage.
"Someone left you a letter
at the box office," he says.

Fozzie reads the fan letter out loud.
"Your act with Animal
was the best we have seen."
It is signed by Waldorf and Statler.
"Wow, even those guys who heckle me
liked our act," says Fozzie.
Then the bear reads the rest of the letter.
"P. S. That is the first time we have not
fallen asleep during your show—because
Animal played so loud!"

Waldorf and Statler

"Oh, well!" says Fozzie with a smile.

"That is showbiz!"

"Showbiz!" agrees Animal.